Mine.

Yours.

Written by **Marsha Diane Arnold**

Illustrated by **Qin Leng**

Kids Can Press

Yours.

Yours.

Yours.

Mine.

Yours.

Mine!

Yours!

Mine! Mine! Mine!

Mine!

Mine?

Yours!

OURS!

To Gráinne Charisse, Flint Kelly Oak and Blaise Diane — ours — M.D.A.

To my loves, Lou and Mark — Q.L.

The animals in this book are from Asia. In the order they appear in the story, they are: giant pandas, pangolin, raccoon dog, red panda, fishing cat, river otter, Chinese jumping mice, yellow-throated martens, golden snub-nosed monkey.

Text © 2019 Marsha Diane Arnold
Illustrations © 2019 Qin Leng

Kids Can Press gratefully acknowledges the financial support of the Government of Ontario, through the Ontario Media Development Corporation; the Ontario Arts Council; the Canada Council for the Arts; and the Government of Canada for our publishing activity.

Published in Canada and the U.S. by Kids Can Press Ltd.
25 Dockside Drive, Toronto, ON M5A 0B5

Kids Can Press is a Corus Entertainment Inc. company

www.kidscanpress.com

The artwork in this book was rendered in pen and ink and watercolor.
The text is set in Catalina Typewriter.

Edited by Yvette Ghione and Debbie Rogosin
Designed by Marie Bartholomew

Printed and bound in Shenzhen, China, in 10/2018 by C & C Offset

CM 19 10 9 8 7 6 5 4 3 2 1

LIBRARY AND ARCHIVES CANADA CATALOGUING IN PUBLICATION

Arnold, Marsha Diane, author
    Mine, yours / written by Marsha Diane Arnold ; illustrated by Qin Leng.

ISBN 978-1-77138-919-8 (hardcover)

    I. Leng, Qin, illustrator II. Title.

PZ7.A7363Mi 2019   j813'.54   C2018-902093-8